Patchwork Dog and Calico Cat

Greta Burroughs

DEDICATION

This book is dedicated to my husband, Robert F. DeBurgh
who originated the characters of Patchwork Dog and Calico
Cat in a poem he wrote. He graciously let me steal his idea.

PATCHWORK DOG AND CALICO CAT
Robert F. DeBurgh

Patchwork Dog and Calico Cat
Lived their lives in a constant spat,
All day long it was tit for tat
With the Patchwork Dog and the Calico Cat.

They would chase each other round and round
In and out and up and down,
The noise they made was a terrible sound
Barking, meowing, knocking things down.

Oh be quiet, don't do that
You silly dog, you silly cat,
That was said from way down low
By a mouse in the house don't you know.

A decent mouse can't get any rest
With you two being such a pest,
All this fighting makes no sense
There's nothing to say in its defense.

So why don't you two just be friends
And let this silly squabble end,
Let all this useless fighting cease
And in this house we will have peace.

CONTENTS

Acknowledgments   i

1   Can Dogs Fly?   1

2   Rain, Rain, Go Away   8

3   What's in the Box?   19

4   Wishes Can Come True   27

5   Dogs Can Fly   35

Other Books by Greta Burroughs   43

About the Author   46

ACKNOWLEDGMENTS

Thanks Donna for the time and effort you put into helping me finish up this project. I want to thank Phyllis Reyes and Vickie Johnstone for being my beta readers.

I also want to thank Nickie Storey-Bailey and her daughter, Sydney. I appreciate the feedback from a child's point of view.

Special thanks go to my husband, Robert F. DeBurgh for his patience and guidance in helping me with my writing. I could not do it without him.

1 CAN DOGS FLY?

Patchwork Dog and Calico Cat are the best of friends. They eat together, sleep together and best of all, play together.

They were not always friends though. When they first met, they did not like each other at all.

They used to bite each other's ears and pull each other's tail. The two little guys were very sad and did not understand why.

One day the house mouse explained things to them. "All day long you two run around here making all kind of noise, barking, meowing, and breaking things."

"I can't get any rest. All this fighting doesn't make any sense. Why don't you try being friends?" said the little mouse.

Patchwork Dog and Calico Cat really did not like to fight, so they decided to follow house mouse's advice and gave friendship a try.

It was not easy at first, but soon they realized that being friends was a lot more fun and a lot less painful.

Best of all, the two friends were now happy and enjoyed playing together.

All day long, back and forth, in and out, tumbling, wrestling and chasing each other until they were so tired they couldn't move.

One warm spring day the two friends were resting under a large shade tree, watching the birds flying in and out of the top branches.

Patchwork Dog loved to chase birds. That was one of his favorite games. But the birds were up too high for him to reach.

"I wish I could fly," said Patchwork Dog, "then I could chase the birds no matter how high they go. Why not? It can't be too hard. If a little bird can do it, a big dog like me can do it too."

Calico Cat just sat and watched her silly friend jumping around, flapping his front legs up and down, and wagging his tail so fast that his back end did lift off the ground.

After a while, Patchwork Dog plopped down on the ground panting. He was so tired. He was ready to give up on his idea of flying.

Calico Cat liked to play tricks on her not too smart friend. With a mischievous smile on her face she said, "You need some help, Patchy. If you run as fast as you can down that hill over there, jump up into the air, then pump your legs and wag your tail, maybe you will fly."

Patchwork Dog looked at the hill and thought about it.

"Yeah! Maybe you are right, Calico. I'll go to the top of the hill, and run as fast as I can down the hill and jump in the air. Then I'll flap my legs, wag my tail and I'll fly!"

Calico Cat watched the silly dog get into position. She waited and waited but Patchwork Dog just stood there.

"What's the matter, Patchy? Are you going to fly or not?"

Patchwork Dog looked down the long steep hill, "It's a long, long way down to the bottom. I don't know about this."

Calico Cat laughed and said, "You can't fly. You're a dog. You don't have wings. Birds can do it, but you can't."

Well this made Patchwork Dog mad. He didn't like being told he could not do something, and he really didn't like it when Calico laughed at him.

"Grrrr...I'll show that cat. I'll go to the top of the hill and get a running start, jump into the air, and I'll show her that I can fly better than any bird."

4

At the top of the hill, Patchwork Dog started running.

He got faster and faster and FASTER.....

By the time he got to the steepest part of the hill, the little dog was running so fast that his feet left the ground and he was sailing through the air.

"I'm flying, I'm flying."

He pumped his legs and wagged his tail but something was wrong. His flying speed got slower and slower and then...

PLOP!!!! Flat on the ground.

Calico Cat ran over to her friend. "Patchy, Patchy are you OK?"

It took a few seconds, but Patchwork Dog looked up and said, "I think I'll leave flying to the birds. Soaring through the air is fun but the landing hurts too much."

Patchwork Dog slowly stood up and walked around, checking to make sure his legs still worked the way they were supposed to.

Patchy could have been hurt very badly trying to fly like a bird, but luckily all he got were some bumps and bruises.

He learned a valuable lesson that day. Be happy with who you are and leave the flying to those who know how to do it.

"All this flying has made me hungry. Let's go in and see if supper is ready," said the tired little puppy.

So the two friends went back home to eat and get a good nights sleep so they would be ready for a new adventure tomorrow.

Greta Burroughs

Calico Cat

What do you think about the trick Calico played on Patchy? Was it a mean trick or just fun?

Have you ever wished you could fly like a bird?

Do you think Patchy will remember the lesson he learned?

2 RAIN, RAIN, GO AWAY

One hot summer afternoon, Patchwork Dog and
Calico Cat were sitting under a large shade tree
beside a big lake.

Patchwork Dog was soaking wet since he had taken a swim in the lake.

"Calico, why don't you jump in the lake? It's fun splashing around and the water will cool you off."

"Getting all wet is no fun, Patchy. It's too much like taking a bath, and I do not like taking baths."

Calico Cat stood up and stretched. "I'd rather go home. It's nice and cool in our house and I'm ready for a nap in my comfortable bed."

She knew that Patchy would not like this idea so she started walking away before he could say anything.

Patchwork Dog was not too excited about going home. He was in no hurry to follow his friend so he ran around sniffing all of the bushes, flowers and trees.

He didn't notice the storm clouds forming above them, but Calico did.

"Patchy, what are you doing? It looks like we might get a thunderstorm and I want to get home before it rains. Come on!"

Patchwork sighed and said, "OK Calico. I don't know why you are in such a hurry. There are so many things to look at and smell around here."

"Look over here. There are some animal footprints I've never seen before. I wonder who made them."

The curious dog started walking with his nose glued to the ground, following the footprints.

"Our house is the other way, Patchy. You're going the wrong way."

Patchwork Dog pretended not to hear his friend. He kept walking away from Calico Cat and disappeared into Mr. Smith's cornfield.

"Patchy, you come back here right now!!"

A few raindrops started to splatter on the ground in front of the angry cat.

"Patchy, it's starting to rain." No answer from the dog.

"Patchy!!!" still no answer.

Calico didn't know if she should follow her friend or go home. The rain kept falling and her fur was starting to get wet.

"That dog makes me so mad. I should just leave him and let him find his own way home. Because of him, I'm all wet and very unhappy."

Calico heard something. It sounded like someone calling her name.

She was already soaking wet from the rain, so the soggy cat shrugged her shoulders and started following Patchy's trail into the cornfield.

She walked and walked through the rows of corn, and finally came out the other side.

The two friends had never been on Mr. Smith's farm before, so Calico didn't know exactly where she was.

She looked around and saw the house with some chickens walking around in the front yard. She also saw a big barn with all kinds of tractors and other machines she didn't recognize.

In the side yard was a tool shed and walking beside it was Patchy.

Patchwork Dog still had his nose glued to the ground following the footprints that led him there. He was headed towards the open door of the tool shed.

Calico wanted to get out of the rain so she ran over to the little building and went inside the door.

The little dog did not see Calico until he made his way to the door where the wet, dripping, soggy cat was standing.

"What took you so long, Calico? I've been waiting for you!"

Then he took a closer look at the cat. "Calico, you're all wet! I thought you didn't like being wet."

Patchwork Dog had been so busy following the strange footprints that he didn't realize that it was raining and he was just as wet. He was not a very smart dog.

Calico Cat was so mad she wanted to scream. Just as she was starting to open her mouth, a loud clap of thunder boomed overhead.

The frightened cat forgot all about being mad. She grabbed Patchy and hugged up to him as close as she could get.

Calico did not like thunderstorms. The thunder and lightning were just too much for her to bear, and she started crying.

"Patchwork Dog, why didn't you follow me home? We could be there right now safe and dry in our house. I'm so scared," she cried.

I'm sorry, Calico. I'll just close the door and we'll be OK."

The little dog pushed on the door and it slammed shut. Then he wrapped his paws around the shaking cat and they waited out the storm in Mr. Smith's tool shed.

The thunderstorm did not last too long. The rain stopped pouring down and the thunder wasn't so loud anymore.

"Can we go home now?" Calico whispered. She was afraid that if she talked too loud the storm might hear her and come back.

Patchwork Dog walked over to the door and tried to open it. It was stuck tight.

"Aaah Calico, I think we have a small problem," said the dog.

"Oh no Patchy, we're locked in. What are we going to do? I want to go home." Calico started crying again.

Patchwork Dog didn't like to see his friend so upset, so he ran around looking for another way out of the tool shed.

He tried the windows to see if they would open - no luck. He tried the door again - it wouldn't budge. He even checked all the walls to see if there were any holes they could fit through - still no luck.

The little dog had to do something to cheer up his friend, but what? He tried to think; nothing, no ideas. He was ready to give up.

Then a voice boomed out, "Well you've done it to us now. We're all stuck in here and we'll have to wait for Mr. Smith to come and open the door."

Patchy and Calico looked at each other. They didn't know whether to be scared or glad to have this unexpected company.

"Will you two stop making so much noise and let a skunk sleep in peace?

All this crying and running around is driving me crazy," complained the skunk.

Patchy and Calico looked at each other again. The voice was coming from inside a box on the other side of the room. A black head appeared over the top of the box and continued talking.

"I had to hide in here because of that silly dog following me."

The skunk jumped out of the box and slowly walked towards the two friends.

There was no place for Patchwork Dog and Calico Cat to hide so they just stood there, and watched the skunk getting closer and closer.

"I'm sorry, Mr. Skunk. I didn't mean any harm. I just wanted to find out who made those interesting footprints," said the frightened dog.

"Well now you know. Now we are all stuck in here since you slammed the door shut," said the grouchy skunk. "By the way, my name is Tom."

"It's nice to meet you, Tom," said Calico. "What do we do now?"

"WHAT DO WE DO? ......WE SLEEP," yelled the grumpy skunk.

"I'm hungry and I want my nice, comfortable bed," whined the unhappy cat.

"You can eat when we get out of here, and make a bed like I did," said the skunk as he walked back to his box. "Now be quiet and let me sleep." Tom jumped back in his box.

Patchy and Calico had no choice. They didn't want to make the grouchy skunk angry.

The two friends knew about the terrible, stinky spray that skunks have and didn't want to take the chance of being squirted with that nasty stuff. So they gathered some old rags together and made a bed.

It wasn't as comfortable as their beds at home, but it was better than sleeping on the floor.

The two friends didn't have a very good night. It was too warm in the tool shed. They were very uncomfortable on the hard floor, and the skunk snored like a freight train.

Finally, it was morning and they awoke to the sound of the tool shed door opening.

Mr. Smith looked through the door and saw the two hideaways sleeping on the bed of rags. He didn't see Tom because the skunk was still hiding in his box.

"It looks like I have some visitors," said Mr. Smith. "I'm sure someone at your house is very worried about you. Run on home now before it's too late to get your breakfast."

That is just what the two friends did. They ran all the way home and didn't stop until they were at their front door.

All they could think about was having a nice breakfast and curling up in their beds.

When they got home, everything was just as they wished. Breakfast was already prepared in their bowls and their beds were right where they left them.

Patchy and Calico were not used to missing supper and were very hungry, so they wasted no time eating every bite of food and licking the bowls clean.

Now it was time for bed. The two companions curled up in their nice soft blankets and did not move again for a long, long time.

Sweet dreams.

Have you ever smelled

a skunk?

Do you think Tom the skunk got out of Mr. Smith's shed safely?

Are you afraid of thunderstorms?

Will this lesson teach Patchy to be more careful when he is searching for new adventures?

3 WHAT'S IN THE BOX?

It was a cool, crisp autumn day. Patchwork Dog and Calico Cat were out for their daily walk.

Patchy was bored. He had not had any adventures lately and the little dog wanted to do something exciting.

Calico was happy. She didn't care too much for adventures. As long as her day was calm and quiet, the cat was content.

Unfortunately for Calico, today was not going to be calm or quiet.

Patchwork Dog was leading the way. That was a big mistake. He heard people talking and wanted to see what was going on.

The two friends quietly crept up and hid behind some bushes. They wanted to see, but did not want anyone to see them.

"Look Calico," whispered Patchwork Dog, "they are loading boxes into the back of the truck. I wonder what's in the boxes."

"Patchy, we are not going over there to look." Calico Cat gave her friend a stern look and sat down. "I am not leaving this spot!"

"Calico, you are no fun. Don't you want to know what's in the boxes? It might be something to eat. It's been a long time since breakfast and I'm hungry."

Calico had to agree that she was maybe a little bit hungry too, but she did not want anyone to see them sneaking around.

"OK Patchy. There are some boxes still on the ground over there next to the trees. We can stay behind all these bushes, and go around and look in them."

The two companions slowly and quietly tiptoed around, hiding behind the bushes and trees until they were close to the boxes.

Patchwork Dog peeked out between two bushes to see if the coast was clear.

"I don't see anybody," whispered the little dog. "Let's go."

Patchy stuck his head out and took another good look around.

Then the brave little dog inched his way out of the bushes a little more... and a little more... and a little more until he was all the way out of their hiding place.

Calico poked her head through the bushes and watched her friend. She was too scared to leave their hiding place.

"Go ahead Patchy and look in the boxes. I'll stay right here and keep a look out for anyone coming."

Patchy was a little scared too, but he just had to take a quick look. He lay flat on the ground and crawled...

slowly... carefully... until his nose was touching the bottom of one of the boxes.

He looked to the left... he looked to the right...he looked behind him...nobody around.

Patchwork Dog slowly stood up until his nose was level with the top of the box.

The curious little dog peeked into the box...

Apples, lots of red juicy apples - Patchwork Dog loved apples.

He was so excited that he did not hear someone coming up behind him until it was too late.

Crack... crunch... the footsteps got closer. Patchy didn't know what to do. He was so scared that he couldn't stop shaking.

The footsteps stopped. Then all was quiet.

"Oh no," thought the frightened little dog, "I'm in big trouble."

Patchwork Dog felt a tap on his shoulder. He turned around and saw...

Calico Cat.

"Gotcha Patchy!!" The cat started laughing and dancing around. She didn't get to play tricks on her friend very often, so she was really enjoying this.

Needless to say, Patchwork Dog didn't think it was all that funny.

He started chasing Calico around and around the boxes. That went on until they were both so tired they couldn't run anymore.

"That was a mean trick you played on me, Calico," panted the tired dog.

"Oh Patchy, I saw all of the people leave in the trucks, so I thought I'd have a little fun," giggled the silly cat. "By the way, what's in the box?"

With all the excitement, Patchwork Dog had forgotten all about his discovery.

Now he brightened up and replied, "Apples, lots and lots of apples. Are you as hungry as I am?"

Both of them had worked up quite an appetite. Without another word they both started eating and eating and eating.

By the time they were finished, there were apple cores everywhere.

The two friends had eaten so many apples. All they could do now was lie down and take a nap.

When Patchwork Dog woke up, he had a terrible stomach ache. Calico Cat was moaning and groaning, and rolling around on the ground. She was sick too.

"Patchy, I feel terrible. Why did I eat so many apples?"

"Me too, Calico, I am never going to eat another apple again!"

"It's getting late and we need to be getting home," said the little dog. "Can you walk?"

Calico stood up and took a few steps. "Yes, but it's going to be a long walk home."

The two miserable animals started the long trek home. This was the first time Patchy did not make any stops to check out any new smells.

Step by step, they slowly made their way home. The two sick friends had to stop and rest a couple of times along the way.

They were so miserable. Oh what a terrible stomach ache!

It seemed to take forever, but they finally made it home. The two friends walked right past their supper bowls and went straight to their beds, and didn't move again until the next morning.

Patchwork Dog and Calico Cat learned a valuable lesson today, but will they remember it tomorrow?

Do you like

Apples?

What was the lesson Patchy and Calico learned in this story?

Have you ever had a stomach ache?

Calico played another trick on Patchy did you think it was funny?

4 WISHES CAN COME TRUE

Patchwork Dog and Calico Cat were out for their morning walk. The sun was a bright, fiery ball in the sky, and it was hot, too hot.

The two friends decided to lie down in the shade of a big oak tree to rest for a little while and cool off.

"You know, Calico, I'm getting tired of walking everywhere we go. People have it easy. They have cars and trucks to take them places. All we have is our four feet," complained the unhappy little dog.

"Wouldn't it be nice to ride somewhere? Feel the wind ruffling my fur... my ears flapping in the breeze... to magically go anywhere I want to go and never get tired feet."

"Dream on Patchy. I would love to be able to go places curled up and comfortable in the back seat of a car." Calico sighed and then continued in a sad voice, "but I don't think it will ever happen."

The two dreamers had been told that if they really wanted something and wished really hard for it to happen, their dreams could come true. So that's what they did.

Calico and Patchy relaxed and slept in their cool, shady spot, imagining what it would be like to be magically transported wherever they wanted to go.

BANG!! WHOMP!! WHOMP!!! WHOMP!!!!

Patchwork Dog and Calico Cat jumped up, wide awake. "What was that?" cried the scared cat.

They looked around, trying to find the source of the terrible noise.

They noticed a truck going very slowly down the road. Something was wrong with the truck.

One of the tires did not look right and was making the whomping noise. The truck stopped and the driver got out.

"That looks like Farmer Gray," said Patchy. "Let's go down and see if he is OK."

The curious dog ran off without waiting for an answer and as usual Calico followed.

Patchwork Dog ran straight to the truck, and skidded to a stop. The little dog sniffed at the flat tire, then looked up to Farmer Gray and asked in his own doggy way, "What's the matter?"

By that time, Calico had arrived and she wanted to know too.

Farmer Gray looked at the pair and said, "I don't guess you two can help me change that tire."

He paused for a minute, and then continued, "I didn't think so. Well, will you stay and keep me company while I work?"

Patchwork Dog jumped around and wagged his tail. Calico Cat purred and rubbed against Farmer Gray's leg, both of them saying, "YES, YES, YES."

Farmer Gray chuckled and said, "OK, let's get to work."

The farmer got out all his tools and the spare tire, and carried it all around to where his chore awaited him. The two companions followed him every step of the way, sometimes getting underfoot.

Farmer Gray didn't mind. He just stepped around his helpers, giving each one a friendly pat on the head.

Finally, the job was finished and all the tools were put away. All three of them were totally exhausted and needed a rest, so they walked up to the big oak tree and sat down in the shade.

They sat there for a while, relaxing and cooling off. Farmer Gray sighed and said, "Well guys, you are good helpers and I think you deserve a reward. How about a ride in my truck?"

Patchwork Dog and Calico Cat were so excited that they ran around Farmer Gray, barking, meowing and jumping until the farmer said, "OK you two, come on. Let's go downtown and get a new tire."

Farmer Gray opened the door and the two friends jumped into the truck.

So began the day's grand adventure....

Patchwork Dog and Calico Cat were so happy. Their dreams were coming true.

Calico curled up on the seat and was asleep in a few minutes. Patchy had his head out the window, his ears flapping in the breeze... the wind ruffling his fur... just as he had imagined.

All too soon, they were at the tire store and the companions stayed in the truck while Farmer Gray took care of his business.

Patchy and Calico didn't mind the wait; they were anxiously awaiting the ride back home.

"Calico, you slept through the whole ride and missed everything. Stay awake this time."

"I enjoyed my nap, Patchy. I'll try to stay awake on the way home but I make no promises." Cats love to sleep wherever and whenever they can.

Farmer Gray finished his business and the magical trip home began. It was every bit as wonderful as their first ride.

Calico stayed awake and the two friends saw new sights they never knew existed.

In town, there were stores and houses one right next to the other. There were so many cars and trucks - all different shapes and sizes.

And all the people - men, women and children all walking, talking and going in different directions.

The little dog and cat were getting dizzy looking left and right, trying to see everything. There was so much going on.

It got easier to take in all of the sights and sounds as they left town and rode back into the country. There weren't so many buildings and cars and people, but the ride was just as exciting.

The countryside started looking familiar. Patchwork Dog and Calico Cat were getting close to their home. They were so surprised at how far they had traveled today.

They had never been to town before. It was too far to walk. They had never seen so many people, and cars and trucks in one place before.

This had been one of the most exciting days they had ever had.

When Farmer Gray stopped at their house, the two friends jumped out of the truck. Patchwork Dog barked and ran around the yard announcing his arrival back home.

Calico Cat was a little more dignified. She slowly walked from the truck to the front door of the house. She wanted everyone to see her make her grand entrance.

Farmer Gray drove away and the two happy friends went inside their house.

Nothing could make this day any better. It really was a dream come true.

What is your

favorite dream?

Greta Burroughs

Do you believe that if you wish hard enough that your dreams could come true too?

If you had three wishes, what would they be?

Have you ever had a flat tire while riding in a car? Did it make the whomping noise?

Have you ever seen a flat tire?

5 DOGS CAN FLY

Patchwork Dog and Calico Cat woke up bright and early, one chilly winter morning, ready for a new adventure.

"Where should we go today, Calico? It's a perfect day to go exploring."

"Oh no, Patchy, I know that look in your eyes. When you look at me like that, we usually get in trouble."

"When have I ever gotten you in trouble, Calico? I just want to have some fun today."

"Fun... like sneaking into Mr. Smith's tool shed and being locked in there all night?

... or like eating all those apples and being sick for two days?

or like...

"OK! OK! We have been in a few jams, but think of it as a way to learn new things."

"Yeah, we learned never to do things like that again," said Calico Cat.

"See," said the proud little dog, "if we didn't have any adventures, we would never learn valuable lessons."

"Oh well, what do you have in mind to learn today?" grumbled the cat.

Patchwork Dog ran around the yard, looking for something new and exciting. He climbed up the hill and looked around, and then he found it.

"Calico, come here and tell me what you see over there."

Calico Cat walked over to where her friend was standing and cautiously looked in the direction in which Patchy was pointing.

"All I see are trees, the stream and a big, empty field."

"No Calico, look up in the sky."

"What is that? It's too big to be a bird," exclaimed the surprised cat.

"Calico Cat, I'm surprised you don't know what an airplane looks like. That's Mr. Wilson's airplane."

"Patchy, remember what happened the last time you tried to fly? You ran down that big hill, started flying, and then fell flat on your face."

Patchwork Dog replied, "I don't want to fly, I just want to look at the airplane. Come on, let's go."

With that the dog ran down the hill towards Mr. Wilson's big, grassy field.

"Oh my," said Calico Cat, "I guess I better go with him. There's no telling what trouble that silly dog will get into if he goes by himself." And off went the cat, following her friend.

When they arrived at the field, Patchy and Calico hid behind some tall bushes, and watched as the airplane came in for a landing.

"Look at that, Calico, the airplane is falling out of the air. Look out, Mr. Wilson!" cried Patchwork Dog.

Just as the two friends were starting to run away, the airplane lifted its nose… the wheels touched the ground…and the airplane rolled to a stop next to a large building.

They watched as Mr. Wilson climbed out of the airplane.

"Mr. Wilson is going into that big building. Look, he left the door open on the airplane," said Patchwork Dog.

"You are not going over there," said the surprised cat.

"Just a quick look, Calico, I want to see the inside of the airplane. I promise I'll come right back."

Then off ran the curious dog before Calico could say anything more.

When Patchwork Dog got close to the airplane, he walked very slowly and carefully. He hid behind one of the wheels and looked around.

He didn't hear anything or see anybody so he quietly crept over to the open door, and peeked in.

"Wow there's a lot of strange buttons, knobs and pedals in there. I wonder what they are all for?"

He stretched his paw as far as he could but couldn't quite reach anything.

"Maybe if I jump up and down…"

The bouncing dog still couldn't touch anything. He jumped a little higher and higher and higher…

BAM! CRASH!! THUMP!

Patchwork Dog jumped too high, bumped his head and then tumbled down onto the ground.

A voice sounded behind him, "Who is messing with my airplane?"

Patchwork Dog was too scared to move. The little dog looked up and saw a very unhappy Mr. Wilson standing beside him.

Mr. Wilson looked at Patchwork Dog and started to laugh. "How could such a little dog make so much noise? Do you like airplanes? Want to go for a ride?"

Patchwork Dog forgot about being so scared. He jumped up off the ground and started running around the airplane, barking with joy.

"OK little boy, hop in and we'll take a short flight around the field."

Patchy was so happy. He jumped in the airplane with Mr. Wilson and before he knew it they were rolling out to the runway.

It was a little scary at first. The airplane was very loud and the noise hurt Patchy's ears.

Plus the ground was uneven and the little dog had to hold on tight so he would not bounce off his seat.

Once they took off and were flying, Patchwork Dog forgot all about being scared. It was wonderful.

Everything looked so different. The houses were so small, people were even smaller. All of the farms and fields were in blocks like a checkerboard.

Patchy did not know which way to look; there was so much to see. He wished Calico could be with him.

But knowing her, she would probably be trembling under the seat. She was such a scaredy cat!

All too soon the flight was over and Mr. Wilson was bringing the plane in for a landing. The airplane felt like it was falling out of the sky, and the ground was getting closer and closer.

Patchy closed his eyes. He did not like this part of the flight.

But Mr. Wilson knew what he was doing. The airplane touched down with a little thump, and then slowly rolled back over to where they had started from, next to the big building.

Mr. Wilson parked the airplane and let the little dog out.

All Patchy wanted to do was run, jump and play. He was so happy.

Today was a very special day. A day he would remember forever....

Have you ever flown in an airplane?

What do you think your neighborhood would look like from way up high in the sky?

Do you think Calico would have enjoyed the flight or would she have been a 'scaredy cat'?

****

OTHER BOOKS BY GRETA BURROUGHS

Gerald and the Wee People (a young adult fiction/fantasy novel)

Two teenagers respond to a plea for help and literally fall into another world. They become involved in a war and invent some clever plans to temporarily prevent the enemy from entering the village of the wee people. Time is running out, the gates are getting weaker and the weapon stash is dwindling. Something else has to be done to stop the war.

Gerald, Vernon and six companions embark on a quest to defeat the crazed forest god who is set on destroying all the inhabitants living on that world. They follow a path described in an old prophecy but things do not go as planned.

House on Bo-Kay Lane (book two in the Wee People series; will be available in summer, 2012)

Gerald and Vernon believe their time with the wee people came to an end after they returned to their home world but begin to wonder when strange things started to happen at an abandoned house in their neighborhood. Ghostly images of familiar faces from the wee people village are seen in the windows, echoes of voices from the past haunt the boys' dreams and an undeniable curiosity draws Gerald and Vernon to investigate the mysterious haunted house. What they find takes them back to the world of the wee people and a new adventure begins.

Heartaches and Miracles (a non-fiction account of my experiences with an autoimmune disorder called ITP)

Heartaches and Miracles is a combination biography, research information and pep talk for anyone suffering with ITP or for family members and friends who want to understand what this disease is all about. There are excerpts from other ITPers who have been on or are still on the never ending roller coaster ride of steroids, surgery and other types of medications and treatments. There are no cures for ITP or for any autoimmune disorder for that matter. The treatments and medications can have terrible side effects, but the disease can be controlled in most people. It can be a hard road filled with relapses and disappointments but with a positive attitude and support from friends and family, there is hope. *Heartaches and Miracles* was written as a form of chicken soup for the ITP soul to give encouragement and strength to those affected by this blood disorder. Reading how others have coped, hopefully will give those newly diagnosed a glimpse of what to expect and give everyone with ITP a new hope for tomorrow.

ABOUT THE AUTHOR

Greta Burroughs loves to read. No matter where she is, there is always a book close at hand. Her love of reading began at an early age and blossomed over time to include many different genres, her favorite now being fantasy.

As a preschool and elementary school teacher, Greta tried to instill the joy of reading in the children she worked with. Books were an important part of her classroom and story time was the highlight of the day.

It has been a while since Greta was in a classroom but she had lots of experience in reading to children of various ages and remembers what they enjoyed listening to. She tries to incorporate that knowledge into her work as an author and believes it makes her a better writer of children's books.

The adventures in *Patchwork Dog and Calico Cat* were written several years before the book was published. The manuscript was put away while she concentrated on her career as a freelance journalist and before that in aviation education. When medical issues kept her from being able to work outside the home, the writing bug hit her and the old manuscript was dusted off, rewritten, illustrated and published.

Greta's one nonfiction narrative, *Heartaches and Miracles* describes the roller coaster ride she has been on fighting an autoimmune disorder called ITP. She has also published a young adult fiction fantasy novel entitled *Gerald and the Wee People* and has plans to write a sequel to that called *The House on Bo-Kay Lane.* That is not the end of her literary itinerary; Greta has several other children's book in mind for the future.

Greta Burroughs

6294582R00033

Printed in Great Britain
by Amazon.co.uk, Ltd.,
Marston Gate.